BEAT YOUR GREENS

Adapted by Laura Dower from the
"Beat Your Greens" storyboards by Paul Rudish

Based on "THE POWERPUFF GIRLS,"
as created by Craig McCracken

SCHOLASTIC INC.

New York   Toronto   London   Auckland   Sydney
Mexico City   New Delhi   Hong Kong

ISBN 0-439-25179-6

Cover designed by Peter Koblish
Interiors designed by Maria Stasavage
Illustrated by Ken Edwards

12 11 10 9 8 7 6 5 4 3 2 1   1 2 3 4 5 6/0

Printed in the U.S.A.
First Scholastic printing, May 2001

THE CITY OF TOWNSVILLE!
On planet Earth . . .
Out in outer space . . .

Just behind Earth's moon, a mysterious spacecraft lies in . . . wait! That ship's launching a spore-pedo!

In a flash, a strange space-pod crash-lands on Earth! It explodes in a superspore cloud that spreads across miles of farmland in Farmsville.

And all night long, as the field of wholesome natural foods grows . . .

the creepy space-pod glows . . .

and glows . . . and glows!

The next morning, Farmsville is ready to rise and shine! These humble residents grow and farm wholesome natural foods! They harvest, pack, ship, and deliver truck-loads of the stuff.

Where are the foods heading? To the hungry residents of Townsville, of course!

And all over Townsville, moms and dads get kids to eat up all those farm-grown greens ... right?

Not quite!

Eat your vegetables!

I don't eat broccoli!

No eat bock - lo - ree!

Jeez! Broccoli is for sissies!

Woo! Woo! Here comes the broccoli express!

Hey! The Powerpuff Girls don't like the icky green stuff, either.

"That is definitely not cake," says Blossom.

"Nope. And it ain't a corn dog," says Buttercup.

"I know it's not a hamster, either," says Bubbles.

"WHAT?" Blossom and Buttercup cry. "YOU EAT HAMSTERS?"

"Nooooo! I *like* hamsters . . . and I know I *don't like* that!" Bubbles explains.

"Now, Girls, it's exactly what growing superheroes need to charge their powers! It's packed with vitamins and minerals!" says the Professor.

"But it tastes *nasty*!" Buttercup says.

"Well, Girls, you're not leaving the table until the broccoli is all gone! The only way to get rid of your broccoli is to eat it all up — " And with that, Professor Utonium took a big bite . . . .

Meanwhile, back in outer space . . . The aliens who sent the glowing space-pod have moved on to the next stage of their evil plan. These Broccoloids want to make Earth part of their empire!

WEED OUT THE HUMAN BEANS!

"Initiate the hypnotransmithysiser so that Earth's barbaric mammal-people shall be hypnotized into a vegetable state! My warriors will weed out all the human beans so we can harvest the fruits of Earth and plant the seeds of a brand-new empire! HEH! HEH! HEH!"* cackles the Broccoloid leader.

Translation: Let's take over Earth NOW!

Back in Townsville, something's really wrong with the Professor. Could it be . . . *the broccoli?*

"See, I told ya that stuff was way wrong!" Buttercup groans.

"Why'dja eat it, Professor? Why? Why?" Bubbles moans.

"Wait!" Blossom says. "Do you hear that noise? Cries for help! It sounds like we're not the only ones in trouble!"

The Powerpuff Girls head out over Townsville to figure out what's going on.

Everywhere they look, kids are crying! Moms and dads had taken bites of broccoli and zonked out. Now everyone has the same eerie green glow. . . .

"Just like the Professor!" Blossom declares. "We've gotta investigate that broccoli!"

The Girls trace the broccoli all the way back to its roots in Farmsville.

"Hey, Girls, over here!" Blossom's found the source.

"Looks like a missile," says Buttercup.

"Or a weird pea pod," adds Bubbles.

"Or both!" Blossom looks a little closer. Her microscopic vision reveals what's hidden inside the pod. Alien mind-control spores!

"There's spores all over this field," Buttercup says, looking around.

"It must have infected all our broccoli," Blossom decides.

"But where did it come from?" Bubbles wonders.

And just then . . .

15

"What are you Earth creatures doing here?" the Broccoloid emperor yells. "Why aren't *you* hypnotized?"

Blossom's got the answer. "'Cause we didn't eat none of your diabological spores."

With that, the Broccoloid leader orders his warriors to attack the Powerpuff Girls — *pronto*!

But every time a Broccoloid gets its block knocked off, another one grows in its place!

"Eeeeeeek!" the Powerpuff Girls shriek. How can they beat these greens?

Blossom remembers something smart the Professor once said.... "The only way to get rid of your broccoli is to eat it all up —" And that gives her a big idea.

17

"We gotta eat 'em to beat 'em!"

"Buttercup and Bubbles! Swallow your pride, Girls!"
Blossom cries. "Take a bite of the enemy — or else!"

All the sisters can say is *Eeeeewwww!* But they do it anyway.

They chomp and chew their way through most of the Broccoloid forces.

These aliens are about to be history!

"Oooh! I'm getting full," Bubbles says, rubbing her tummy.

"What? Already?" the Broccoloid leader asks. "Why, you haven't even had the main course yet!"

And in another flash, the Farmsville fields are filled with hundreds of Broccoloid ships.

Now the Powerpuff Girls need help! *Hungry* help!

19

"So you see," Blossom tells a crowd of kids gathered in the middle of Townsville, "the only way to save Earth is to eat broccoli."

20

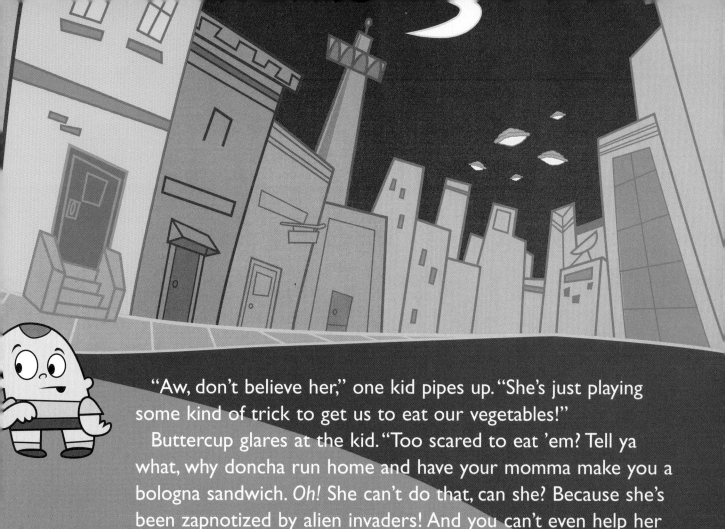

"Aw, don't believe her," one kid pipes up. "She's just playing some kind of trick to get us to eat our vegetables!"

Buttercup glares at the kid. "Too scared to eat 'em? Tell ya what, why doncha run home and have your momma make you a bologna sandwich. *Oh!* She can't do that, can she? Because she's been zapnotized by alien invaders! And you can't even help her out because YOU don't wanna eat a few measly vegetables — "

"OK, STOP!" the kid shouts. "LET'S DO IT!"

And the crowd breaks out into a round of cheers.

So while the Broccoloid forces move together to invade Townsville . . .

The Powerpuff Girls and the kids of Townsville get set to do battle their own way.

And just as the Broccoloids prepare to fire their first lasers on the city . . . Blossom, Bubbles, and Buttercup beat 'em to it! The Powerpuff Girls use their super X-ray vision to zap the Broccoloids' artillery tanks.

Now, the Broccoloid leader sends his foot soldiers to storm the city! But The Powerpuff Girls and the kids are ready and waiting for them, too!

"Release the cheese!" Blossom screams.

In every direction, kids pour pots of melted cheese sauce over that mean broccoli, turning the alien forces into a yummy side dish!

While one crowd of kids gnashes their teeth and noshes the veggies, other Townsville kids have different *snack* attacks!

Kids are jumping out of alleys . . .

Crawling around corners . . .

Sharpening forks and knives . . .

To stop the rest of the Broccoloids bite by BITE!
But the broccoli bad guys keep on coming.

The Powerpuff Girls are getting a little worried. Their kid forces are stuffed full of stalks. They don't know how much more broccoli they can eat!

NOT SO FAST!

But in a flash, the Townsville billy goats motor on through! Hooray! They're making mincemeat out of all the leftover Broccoloid troops.

Now what's a Broccoloid leader to do? His forces are finished!

Blossom, Bubbles, and Buttercup move in closer.

Do they still have room left for one more BITE? *You bet!*

CHOMP

Say good-bye, King Broccoloid!

So with the enemy eaten up, and the parents of Townsville awakened, families are reunited! Normal life resumes!

And The Powerpuff Girls and *all* the kids of Townsville try not to forget something very, very important:

Eat all your vegetables . . . before they beat you!

And so, once again, the day is saved, thanks to The Powerpuff Girls and those hungry little tykes of Townsville!